# DIPS 'N' DOODLES

Written by
Catherine Symons
and
Al Westcott

Illustrated by
Jeanne and Charles Pearson

published by

ODDO PUBLISHING

Mankato, Minnesota

Symbol for
exciting book ideas

1

**managing editor**

Genevieve Oddo

**Advisers**

Anita Bullard
Assistant Professor of English
Oswego State University College, New York

Ruth Foy
Library Coordinator
Baldwin-Whitehall Public Schools
Pittsburgh, Pennsylvania

Jean Henschel
President
Educational Research and Consultation Services
Tucson, Arizona

Norbert C. Lopez
Superintendent of Schools
Espanola, New Mexico

Nina Martin
Coordinator, ESEA Title II
Montgomery, Alabama

Rae Oetting
Minneapolis Public Schools, Minnesota

Mel Schumacher
Coordinator, General Curriculum
Monterey County Board of Education, California

Alvin M. Westcott
Associate Professor of Elementary Education
Oswego State University College, New York

Reading Consultant
William E. Jones
Director of Education
D'Youville College
Buffalo, New York

JS9884di

Michael thought he would burst with excitement before Christmas arrived. Would Santa remember the special things he wanted? The days before Christmas crept by at a turtle's pace. At last the early morning sun of December twenty-fifth spread its yellowness about Michael's bedroom. He scrambled down the stairs, his wide eyes flashing with excitement. His mother, dad and sister Toni followed him down the stairs.

From the doorway of the living room Michael saw several piles of boxes. Each box was wrapped in bright Christmas ribbon with a name tag attached to it. But Michael hurried right past the boxes. He would open them later. Something more interesting had caught his eye. Under the Christmas tree was the skiing equipment he wanted so much. A tag attached to the skis read: "From Mother and Dad."

Michael carefully examined each piece of new skiing equipment. There were new skis, ski boots and ski poles. In addition, there were new ski pants and a ski parka. The ski parka had a large fur hood with fur cuffs on the sleeves.

Michael put on all of his new skiing equipment. He waddled across the living room to the big mirror and stared at himself.

"You look like a furry penguin," said his mother. Furry Michael shook with laughter. "Your father and I have arranged for you to have a few skiing lessons. We hope you will enjoy them."

Michael's eyes lighted with joy.

The next afternoon Michael hurried eagerly to his first skiing lesson.

"Hello, young fellow," said the ski teacher. "My name is Mister Jingle."

"I'm Michael," Michael replied. Michael looked up at Mister Jingle who was standing in the doorway of the ski lodge. Mister Jingle was very big, very tall. Michael was eight years old; very sturdy, but small when he stood next to Mister Jingle.

"Why do boys and girls call you Mister Jingle?" asked Michael.

"I'm glad you asked that question. The reason is quite simple. I have a pair of fancy ski boots that have bells on them. The bells jingle when I ski. I don't have them on today but I do have a Swiss bell on top of my cap." Mister Jingle shook his tiny Swiss bell so that Michael could hear it ring.

"But now, let us get on with the skiing lesson," Mister Jingle suggested.

First, Mister Jingle showed Michael how to carry his skis. Mister Jingle stood the skis on their heels, bottom to bottom. Then he helped lift the skis to Michael's shoulder.

Putting down his skis, Michael asked, "How should I use my ski poles?"

"Ski poles will help you to keep your balance," Mister Jingle said. "You can use them to climb hills. If you fall, you can use them to help you get up again. Good skiers use their ski poles to help them make fancy turns," explained Mister Jingle. "Before we try to ski, there is something we should do to our skis," Mister Jingle added. "It will help us to ski faster because it reduces friction."

"Oh, let me guess," coaxed Michael. "Are you going to put grease on the skis so we can slip down the hill faster?"

Mister Jingle laughed. "Well, in a way you are right," he replied. "We use something like grease. It is a special wax." Mister Jingle showed Michael how to wax his skis.

Mister Jingle helped Michael to snap on his skis. Then they shuffled to the base of a small hill behind the ski lodge.

"I feel like I have big feet," shouted Michael excitedly.

Mister Jingle waited at the base of the hill while Michael climbed the hill a few feet until he could go no farther. Then he began to slide backward. Down the hill came Michael, backward! He could not stop at the bottom of the hill and fell sideward into a large snowbank.

One of Michael's legs stuck out of the snow straight up in the air. So did one of his arms and a ski pole. The rest of him was under the snow. Mister Jingle walked over to help pull Michael out of the snowbank.

"It looks like you should learn a safe way to fall," said Mister Jingle with a laugh.

Michael was surprised to hear that a skier should learn how to fall.

"If you learn to fall right," explained Mister Jingle, "you may not get hurt. When you feel you are going to fall, try to fall on your side like this." Mister Jingle showed Michael how to fall safely. "Now you try falling on your side, Michael," said Mister Jingle.

Michael practiced falling several times. Mister Jingle taught Michael how to use his ski poles to get up after a fall.

Mister Jingle showed Michael two different ways to go up a hill on skis: the side step and the herringbone. Michael's skis made a tweed-like pattern in the snow when he did the herringbone.

"You have done well today, Michael," said Mister Jingle. "Your first skiing lesson is over."

"But I haven't done any skiing yet," Michael said sadly.

"Cheer up, Michael. Tomorrow we will do some skiing. Today you learned what are called the basics of skiing." Mister Jingle showed Michael how to wipe off his skis. "Wiping them keeps the snow and ice from crusting on them."

That night Michael dreamed he was skiing down a steep mountain. He could feel the wind blowing hard against him as he hurtled down the hill. It nearly took his breath away. Suddenly a large tree loomed in front of him in his dream. One of his skis was headed toward one side of the tree. His other ski headed toward the other side of the tree. Michael was headed into the middle of the tree. Just as Michael was about to crash into the tree at full speed — THUD!! He fell out of bed onto the hard floor.

"What's all the noise about?" asked Michael's mother as she rushed into his bedroom.

"I guess I was dreaming about skiing," replied Michael as he climbed slowly back into his bed.

"Better to do your skiing on a hill than in bed," his mother said as she tucked the covers under Michael's chin.

The next day Michael hurried to his second skiing lesson. Mister Jingle greeted him at the door of the ski lodge.

Mister Jingle showed Michael how to lean forward and bend his knees while on his skis.

"Now," said Mister Jingle, "I believe you are ready to try skiing down the beginners' hill. It is called 'Bunny Hill.' " Mister Jingle pointed to a small hill beside the ski lodge.

Michael's eyes sparkled as he made his way toward Bunny Hill. He climbed to the top of Bunny Hill using the herringbone. He bent forward on his skis at the top of beginners' hill. Determination was on his face. He pushed off from the top of the hill. Down, down he flew as if his skis were wings. Halfway down the hill Michael's skis hit a bump in the snow. His skis went up and Michael went down. This time Michael used his poles to help himself up again on his skis. He continued skiing to the bottom of the hill.

"Good job," Mister Jingle said, patting Michael gently on his back. "You need more practice, Michael, but you are coming along nicely."

During the next few lessons Mister Jingle helped Michael to perform a step turn. First they tried it together on level snow; then, on a slight slope.

"If you want to turn fast on a hill you may want to use a kick turn," said Mister Jingle. "This turn is made somewhat like kicking a football." He grunted a bit as he performed the kick turn.

"That's pretty tricky," Michael commented after trying several times to kick about on his skis. "I'll stick to the step turn for now. Anyway, I want to go down the hill again."

Again and again, Michael skied down Bunny Hill. With every downhill run he had better control of his skis, except at the bottom of the hill. Each time Michael reached the bottom of the hill, he could not stop reliably. Several times he bumped into something or fell down in order to stop himself. Sometimes he bumped into other skiers. When he did, they all fell down in a big pile of feet and heads and arms and skis.

"That is a large sitzmark you have made," Mister Jingle said as he untangled Michael from two other boys. Michael and the two boys looked bewildered. "The dent made in the snow when a skier falls is called a *sitzmark*," explained Mister Jingle. Mister Jingle showed Michael and the boys how to fill in the sitzmark with snow and pack it down firmly. "There," Mister Jingle said in a pleased voice. "The sitzmark is gone. No skiers will be tripped up by your sitzmark. All good skiers fill in their sitzmarks with snow to keep the slope as smooth and safe as possible.

"It looks as though you need to learn a better way to stop yourself," Mister Jingle said. "Someone may be injured unless you learn a reliable way to stop with your skis."

Michael agreed heartily. Mister Jingle showed him how to point the toes of his skis together as a way of stopping.

"Your skis make the letter 'V' when you want to stop," explained Mister Jingle. "Skiers call this way of stopping the *snowplow*."

"I thought snowplow meant a big truck," Michael replied.

"Most words have more than one meaning, Michael, but there are some words that apply especially to skiing," explained Mister Jingle. "You will learn some skiing words as you learn more about skiing."

"You mean skiers have their own private language?" asked Michael.

"Well, in a way, they do," Mister Jingle replied with a smile. "Most sports have some special words connected with them. Now ski down the hill again, Michael, and try to use the snowplow to stop at the bottom."

"Oh, I'll just fall again," said Michael sadly.

"If you think you can snowplow, you probably will be able to," commented Mister Jingle. "Keep telling yourself you can."

Michael climbed slowly up Bunny Hill. Several boys and Mister Jingle waited at the bottom of the hill to watch Michael ski down. Michael paused at the top of the hill. He looked down at the other boys and Mister Jingle watching him. "I know I can ski down this hill without falling down," Michael said to himself firmly. "They all think I can do it. I can't let them down."

Then he pushed off from the top of Bunny Hill. His skis carried him along slowly at first, then faster and faster and faster. A cold wind blowing up the hill blew flakes of snow onto his nose and eyelashes. Michael partly closed his eyes to block out the sting of the wind. Ahead he could see a bump of snow on the hill.

23

Closer and closer to the bump went Michael. He bent his knees a little more to help get over the bump. He hit the bump at full speed. Up went Michael's skis from the snow. Up went Michael. Off flew Michael's hat.

Down came the skis with Michael still attached to them. For a few seconds he felt as if he were going to fall down. Fighting to keep his balance, he bent forward, then leaned backward, but he did not fall. At the bottom of the hill Michael came to a slow stop using the snowplow.

Mister Jingle and the boys clapped their mittens together with joy.

"That was a fine run," commented Mister Jingle. "Let us all go up to the ski lodge and have a cup of hot cocoa," suggested Mister Jingle. "How about it?"

Michael and his friends agreed and made their way toward the warmth of the ski lodge. Michael really did not need the warm cocoa. Deep down inside he already felt warm because he had mastered Bunny Hill.

From the big window of the ski lodge Michael and his friends watched skiers come down the big slope.

"How does that slope look to you?" asked Mister Jingle.

"Wild and bumpy," replied Michael.

"Well, I think you are ready now to tackle a part of that big slope. Notice how uneven the big slope is. It is one of the trickiest ski slopes in the state," explained Mister Jingle. "It has been named the 'Dips 'n' Doodles' because it has so many bumps and moguls. A *mogul* is a bump made in the snow by skiers turning often in the same spot. It takes a very good skier to come all the way down the Dips 'n' Doodles without falling."

Michael stood, framed by the large window of the ski lodge, watching skiers gracefully gliding down the Dips 'n' Doodles. Long shadows of afternoon reached across the ski slope before Michael became weary of watching the skiers and walked homeward.

The next morning passed slowly for Michael. He could hardly wait for the time of his afternoon skiing lesson to arrive. In his mind he could still see the skiers gracefully gliding down the Dips 'n' Doodles. At last the time for his lesson arrived. He met Mister Jingle at the bottom of the Dips 'n' Doodles.

Michael and Mister Jingle watched skiers being pulled up the Dips 'n' Doodles by the ski tow.

"How does that ski tow work?" asked Michael.

"The skiers hold onto the rope," answered Mister Jingle. "The rope runs on pulleys. The pulleys are turned by a motor. So the motor, together with the rope and pulleys, pulls skiers up the Dips 'n' Doodles."

"It sure is easier than walking up," said Michael with a laugh. "I want to try holding onto the tow-rope," he added.

"All right. Let's try the ski tow," Mister Jingle agreed.

A ski-patrol man and Mister Jingle showed Michael how to hold onto the tow-rope. Up, up, up the hill went Michael and Mister Jingle, pulled by the ski tow.

"Let go of the tow-rope when I give the word," shouted Mister Jingle to Michael above the laughter and shouts of other skiers.

"Now!" called Mister Jingle, and he and Michael dropped off in the snow. Michael regained his balance and looked down the Dips 'n' Doodles. He and Mister Jingle were about halfway up the steep uneven slope.

"It looks like a long way down to the bottom," commented Michael in a shaky voice.

"You may not make it to the bottom without falling the first time you try," Mister Jingle suggested. "But if you keep trying, you can become a fine skier."

He patted Michael firmly on the back. "Now go to it, boy. I'll watch your form."

Michael pushed off with his ski poles and started down the Dips 'n' Doodles. Faster and faster and faster Michael went until he came to the first mogul on the hill.

Michael went over the mogul — head first.

Slowly he picked himself up again. A ski-patrol man asked him if he were hurt. Michael shook his head.

Mister Jingle joined Michael and the ski-patrol man. "Why do you think you fell?" asked Mister Jingle.

"I was going too fast," replied Michael. "I could not control my balance. This Dips 'n' Doodles sure is steep and bumpy."

Mister Jingle pointed to several other skiers. "Notice how those big folks are skiing down the Dips 'n' Doodles?"

"They are going back and forth across the hill," observed Michael, "instead of skiing straight down the hill."

"Exactly right," said Mister Jingle. "Skiing straight down a slope is called *schussing.* Those skiers are zigzagging down the hill. Zigzagging helps a skier to control his speed. It also makes the downhill run longer than skiing straight down the hill. Zigzagging is often called *traversing, parallel skiing,* or *skiing across the slope.*"

"Whoopee! If zigzagging makes a longer ride, I'm going to try it," Michael said quickly, pushing off on his skis.

"Whoa there, boy," cautioned Mister Jingle, at the same time pulling on the end of Michael's stocking cap. "Before you can learn to zigzig you must first learn to turn more reliably on your skis. We can practice turning on our skis tomorrow, Michael. For today's lesson, I think you should spend the remainder of this lesson getting the feel of the lower part of the Dips 'n' Doodles. After skiing down the lower part of the Dips 'n' Doodles a few times you will come to know where every mogul and dip is located."

Michael ageed to spend the remainder of his lesson schussing down the lower part of the Dips 'n' Doodles.

Mister Jingle and the ski-patrol man watched carefully as Michael tried to conquer the tricky slope. They made suggestions to Michael in order to improve his skiing form. Toward late afternoon Michael was able to ski down the lower portion of the Dips 'n' Doodles without falling. This made him very proud.

"You have done very well today," Mister Jingle said to Michael. "Very soon you will be able to start way up there at the top and ski gracefully down without falling. But suppertime is near and I have a surprise for you at the ski lodge."

Michael's eyes lit up with excitement. He teased Mister Jingle for some clues about the surprise. "I won't tell anyone you told me," Michael insisted.

"That sounds familiar," Mister Jingle commented with a laugh. "It will only be a few minutes before we get to the lodge. You can wait that long, can't you?"

"I'm not sure I can," confided Michael. "I might explode before I find out."

Upon reaching the door of the lodge, Michael saw the surprise. Waiting for him inside the ski lodge were his mother, father, and sister, Toni.

"We watched you skiing on the Dips 'n' Doodles, Son. You are learning to ski just fine," his father said with a proud smile.

"You fall a lot," said Toni dryly. "You must be blue and black."

"Every new skier takes some spills," Mother explained to Toni. Then, in a whisper, she added, "Not 'blue and black'; it's 'black and blue.'"

"We thought it would be fun to have supper together here at the lodge tonight," Father said. "Would you like that, Michael?"

"That will be keen," replied Michael.

And so, Toni, Michael, Mother and Father ate supper beside a picture window in the ski lodge. From his seat at the table Michael could see the dancing flames of the log fire burning in the fireplace of the ski lodge. He also could see the dark blue shadows of evening creeping across the Dips 'n' Doodles.

When no one in the family could eat another bite, Father made an announcement: "There is a special reason why your mother and I wanted to have supper with you at the lodge tonight," he explained in a mysterious sounding voice.

Toni and Michael listened carefully.

"The ski-patrol men and the adult skiing club are going to do some torchlight skiing on the Dips 'n' Doodles tonight. Mother and I thought you might like to watch it."

"Would we ever!" exclaimed Michael.

Soon after the late evening sun faded into a cold black sky, skiers bearing flaming torches began skiing down the Dips 'n' Doodles. The bright yellow, orange, red, green, and blue flames from the skiers' torches made dancing streaks down the Dips 'n' Doodles.

Toni, Michael, Father and Mother stood silently in the big window of the ski lodge and watched the swirling colors cascade down the slope.

"You know, Dad," Michael commented, "skiing is more than good exercise. Skiing is a very special way of feeling."

The other skiers watching from the lodge knew exactly what Michael meant.

## ADVICE FOR THE SKIER

Do:

take lessons from an expert skier, if possible, so that you learn to ski properly.

purchase proper skiing equipment and keep it in good condition.

follow directions when using a ski tow or lift.

ski under control.

heed warnings regarding snow conditions.

give downhill skiers the "right of way" when you are climbing uphill.

dress correctly for weather conditions and safety. (Loose-fitting clothing can be dangerous for the skier.)

help other skiers who appear to need help by notifying a ski-patrol man or some other adult.

Don't:

ski alone — especially in remote areas.

walk on the ski runs.

ski too long. (Exhausted skiers are accident prone.)

show off on skis. Show-offs cause many accidents.

try to ski on slopes that overtax your skiing ability.

## about the authors

Catherine Bracco Symons was born in Iron Mountain, Michigan.

Her elementary and secondary education was taken in Illinois and Wisconsin.

In 1951, she received her B.B.A. degree from Mount Mary College, Milwaukee, Wisconsin. In 1954, as a scholarship student, she received her M.A. degree in education from National College of Education, Evanston, Illinois.

She was kindergarten teacher in the Evanston Public School System, Illinois, 1954-1955; in the Appleton School System, Wisconsin, 1959-1966; in the U.S. Naval Air Station, Millington, Tennessee, 1967-1968. She was Principal of the Stephen Foster Elementary School, Appleton, Wisconsin, 1959-1966.

Catherine Bracco Symons has been a member of the National Education Association, Wisconsin Education Association, Wisconsin Elementary School Principals Association, and The Scriptors (Literary Group), Memphis, Tennessee.

She is married to Thomas D. Symons, a member of Kimberly-Clark Corporation, and they have three children.

Alvin M. Westcott was born March 31, 1930 in Mount Kisco, New York. He attended Mount Kisco Elementary School and later graduated from Rome Free Academy in Rome, New York.

Following high school, Alvin M. Westcott attended the State University College at Oneonta, New York. The B.S. degree in Elementary Education was conferred on him in 1955. He then went on to teach in Mount Kisco Elementary School, and the Quaker Ridge School of Scarsdale, New York. In 1957 he was selected to be a graduate fellow in elementary education at Syracuse University at which institution he received his M.S. degree.

Alvin M. Westcott is currently an associate professor of elementary education at State University College, Oswego, New York. He has written and illustrated numerous magazine articles and books.

ODDO books written by Alvin M. Westcott are: Billy Lump's Adventure; Word Bending With Aunt Sarah; Fun With Timothy Triangle; Whispering River (co-author, Catherine Symons); Dips 'n' Doodles (co-author, Catherine Symons); and Rockets and Crackers.

## about the illustrators

Jeanne and Charles Pearson are graduates of Winona State College where they both majored in Art and English. Mr. Pearson is an art teacher and free-lance illustrator in Owatonna, Minnesota where he had worked previously as a scholastic jewelry designer for Josten's, Inc. His main interest is painting North American big game animals.

In addition to illustrating, Jeanne Pearson writes children's books about the Minnesota frontier. She has specialized in painting portraits of children with their horses.

ODDO books illustrated by the Pearsons are: Adventures on Library Shelves, Whispering River, Dips 'n' Doodles, Keiki of the Islands.

The Pearsons have four daughters, a dog, and several ponies and horses.